Kayla and Kugel's Happy Hanukkah

By Ann D. Koffsky

With love and thanks to Mom and Dad,
Rabbi Louis & Hermine Diament,
for all the many Hanukkah memories.
—A.D.K.

Apples & Honey Press
An imprint of Behrman House Publishers
Millburn, New Jersey 07041
www.applesandhoneypress.com

Copyright © 2020 by Ann D. Koffsky

ISBN 978-1-68115-560-9

Library of Congress Cataloging-in-Publication Data

Names: Koffsky, Ann D., author, illustrator.
Title: Kayla and Kugel's happy Hanukkah / Ann D. Koffsky.
Description: Millburn, New Jersey : Apples and Honey Press, [2020] |
Audience: Ages 3-7. | Audience: Grades K-1. | Summary: Young Kayla
celebrates Hanukkah with her family and mischievous dog, Kugel,
by lighting menorahs, playing dreidel, and sharing the
story of how the holiday came to be.
Identifiers: LCCN 2019043794 | ISBN 9781681155609 (hardcover)
Subjects: CYAC: Hanukkah—Fiction. | Family life—Fiction. |
Judaism—Customs and practices—Fiction. | Dogs—Fiction.
Classification: LCC PZ7.K81935 Kg 2020 | DDC [E]—dc23
LC record available at https://lccn.loc.gov/2019043794

Design by Elynn Cohen
Edited by Dena Neusner
Printed in China
1 3 5 7 9 8 6 4 2

I'm Kayla, and this is my dog, Kugel.
We are getting ready for Hanukkah.

I'm looking for the menorahs.
Kugel is helping me.

Kugel!

That's not what we're
looking for.

Kugel, that's not the Hanukkah box—
that's the Purim box!

Okay, you can pretend to be a king.
There's a king in the Hanukkah story too.

Aha! I found the menorahs.
Let's go downstairs and set them up.

Kugel, let's clear this windowsill, so we can put the menorahs here.

Did you know that long, long ago a king said that the Jewish people couldn't celebrate their holidays anymore? "No more Passover! No more Shabbat!" he decreed.

They couldn't go to their Temple. They couldn't light the Temple Menorah.

Its flames used to shine brightly. But now it stood cold and dark.

Kugel, we're using Hanukkah candles
tonight, not Shabbat ones.

Put that away. Please?

Do you want to hear the rest of the story, Kugel? Okay.

The Jewish people fought back—and won!

The king's soldiers ran away, and the Jewish people went to the Temple to light the Menorah.

But the king's soldiers had wrecked the Temple.

And the oil for the Menorah was missing!

The Jewish people had to make everything right again.

Kugel, just because the soldiers made a mess doesn't mean *you* have to.

Finally, they found enough oil
to light the Temple Menorah
for one day.

But the oil lasted for
eight days and nights.

It was a miracle!

That's why we light our Hanukkah menorahs for eight nights.

Come, Kugel—watch us light them.

Kugel, why are you running around and around?

Oh—I get it! You're spinning like a dreidel.

Let's *all* play dreidel.

Happy Hanukkah!

Dear Friends,

Kayla has got it right. Hanukkah is about appreciating how lucky we are to have the freedom to celebrate Jewish holidays, like Passover, Shabbat . . . and Hanukkah itself! Because the Jewish people bravely stood up to the king many years ago, we are all able to celebrate our holidays today.

Kugel has got it right too. Hanukkah is also about playing games and having fun. The letters on the sides of the dreidel are in Hebrew. They stand for Hebrew words that mean "A great miracle happened there." Playing dreidel is one way to celebrate Hanukkah with our families.

After reading the story, talk about these ideas:

What's your favorite thing about Hanukkah? Why?

If you could make up a new game to celebrate the miracle of Hanukkah, what would it be?

Happy Hanukkah,

Ann